Sex in the Air

Let's get buck wild

About the Author,

Lakyshia L. Shelton (Hubert) was born to the parents of Mary L. (Burnett) Shelton and Lorenzo Shelton Sr. in Pahokee Florida; and raised in Clewiston Florida. Lakyshia is the mother of two sons and has currently written Let's Help Each Other Can You Relate to These Stories, My Baby Daddy & The Family Drama That Came Along with It, Poetry of Life Part One and Two, Last but Definitely Not Least Sex in The Strangest Places!

Table of Contents,

Prologue

We lay and play all the time with each other Michelle writes in her diary. Sometimes I enjoy the sex when other times it is over so quickly I wonder why even bother? I mean it's like at first, we'll be laying there kissing and he'll rub all over my body. He kisses me in all my erogenous zones such as my neck and behind my ears. I become instantly aroused and feel the slickness between my legs as he gets on top of me and suck on each of my breast. Then he'll easily slide his penis inside my vagina, oh how good it feels. He asks me "Baby am I hurting you"? I respond "no baby, my vagina is just sucking your penis like a suction cup. About 3 to 5 minutes into the sex things begin to pick up. He starts pounding my vagina just the way I like it. Then soon as I feel myself about to cum or at least getting to the point of climax he moves. I shout, "no baby my nut was coming, I mean damn bae you were at my spot". I'll be just about to cum and he catches his first nut, and everything is over. Sometimes I don't even attempt to try to catch my nut because I already know that by the time he gets his penis in and I start throwing the pussy back he will have nutted. Diary, this is what I begin doing. When he leaves I'll continue laying there wanting my nut, so I slide one finger inside my vagina, holding my lips apart and begin at a slow pace playing with my vagina. I'll take that finger out and suck off the juices and slide it back in. Oh shit, I'm getting closer to my spot. Then I turn over on my belly, spread my legs apart and stick my fingers in as far as I can, then start riding up and down on it. I feel my juices begin to fall down my fingers and I just speed up the pace. Oh, shit you know just what spot to hit. I'm steadily going then I feel a squirt of wetness escape my vagina. I'm shaking and breathing heavily. I lay there for a few minutes and gather myself to take a shower. Now while inside the shower I lay myself on the floor of the shower and put the water where it is flowing directly on my vagina and then stick fingers back inside my vagina. Damn it feels so good to be finger fucking myself. Sounds of my vagina's escaping pleasure as it gets wetter and wetter fills the shower. I begin to swirl my hips, now I'm jabbing my fingers in and out. Shit this feels so good I moan out loud and think to myself damn I have to do this more often. Then I cum again, finish my shower and take a nap. When he got back, and I awakened he burst out and says, "yeah that dick was so good it put you to sleep". I just laughed, looked at my hands, and said "Yes bae you sure did put me to sleep".

Chapter One: Sex on the Porch

Sitting outside on this sunny day I glance aside and there he was to my surprise. He was fine, Hispanic, tall, and built. His lips were pink and juicy like bubble gum in the middle of candy. Every day he would come outside to do his exercise. I watch as he slowly stretches, I wonder what's that bulge in his pants. Then he would holler good morning sweetie before he jogs off. My mind gets so overwhelmed with the thought of his big hands caressing my body. No snap out of it Siearra he would never want anyone like you. Hell, he got a nice paying job, nice car in his yard, and what do you have huh? A minimum wage paying job, your 2006 Nissan continues to break down, and your skin is white. Siearra then says hell my ass is fat and my breast are perky. Sometimes Siearra brings her silver bullet so in the mornings she can just slide it in on vibrate and watch as he squeezes his ass cheeks tightly when he stretches out. One day she got so in tune and didn't realize she let out a moan until she opened her eyes to see he'd stopped what he was doing and was now completely watching her. Oh, I wanted to stop but my body just wouldn't let me. I slid my chair to the screen door and opened it. I untied my robe and my gold lingerie showed. I sat back down and spread my legs, pushed the bullet out, licked it, and put it back in. By this time, he's walking over towards me! When he stepped on the porch he said hello my name is Jose and I'll love to play, he then pushed the chair back and laid me on the floor as he slowly closes the door. Jose grabs the bullet out my vagina and shoves it easily up my ass hole. Jose then slides his tongue in and out my clit. Oh yes baby just how I like it! He removes the bullet from my ass and begins to lick around my ass. I can feel my vagina getting more wet; my eyes begin to roll in the back of my head. Jose stands up and lifts me up! Then say can we go inside; our neighbors have seen enough. My name is Siearra! Jose; and yes, let's go out to the back yard! Once outside Jose takes the sex oil and slowly begins to massage Siearra's body. The oil gets hot as its being rubbed on my back, then all over my ass cheeks. Oh, his hands had such a soft sensational feel. I like a strong man, Siearra whispers in Jose ear! Drop all your clothes and join me in the outdoor tropical hut says Siearra. Siearra serves Jose some chocolate covered strawberries with whip cream from my vagina. Just to have his face that close and lips bumping against my clit slightly made me shiver. Jose lay back as I start to massage his chest with my tongue slowly working my way down until I reach the peak of his penis. I capture his big nine-inch cock inside my mouth and gently suckle on it at first. Then with every stroke of his penis inside and out I suck harder and harder. Then slow and fast again, swallowing his penis and bringing it back out as I am playing with his balls. He quickly pulls out and says you almost made me cum. Then Jose grabs me up and put my back against the wall and tells me to wrap my legs around his waist. I do as I'm instructed while holding him around the neck, when I felt the head slowly sliding in my vagina. I slightly jump with every stroke and he ask Siearra are you ready for this ride?! Yes, yes, I whispered as he steadily picked up the pace. I begin to go up and down with him as he lustfully and hungrily thrust deep inside my vagina. I begin to quiver and moan loudly, oh yes baby fuck me, right there, I'm cumin. Oh, oh yeeeesss I yell as my legs are shaking uncontrollably. Jose say that's right baby cum for me, He then bend me over the chair and push that fat cock right back in my vagina. Jose spread my ass cheeks apart and drops a little spit down my crack and slowly push his pointer and bird fingers in my ass hole. I moan out in pure pleasure as Jose push his fingers in and out. I'm rocking my hips and throwing my ass back. Jose pulls me back close to him while going harder and harder pounding more and more. My legs begin to quiver as I'm getting weaker and weaker, I feel my juices running down my legs as I'm hollering out yes oh shit yes keep fucking me right there. Then I came, Jose turns me around and say open wide as he blows his nut all down my throat. He then goes and run me a bath, picks me up and place me inside the water. It felt so good to have a man, this man whom I had my eyes on cater to my needs. Jose washes my body from head to toe! After I'm finished Jose carries me back to the back yard. We lay out there gazing at the sky, holding each other for as long as we could. The next day Siearra went shopping and to handle a little business. When she arrived back home later that night, she turned soft music on the stereo and begins to prepare her meal. Siearra sauté her bell pepper and onion, then she placed to pieces of steak inside the aluminum foil and poured the onions, bell peppers on the steak wrapped them up and placed them in the oven. Then she wrapped up the potatoes and placed them in the oven. Siearra then cut up some ham, turkey, boiled eggs and made a salad. Then she goes and take a shower, then after she's done she slip into her red see through lingerie! She lotions her legs, and spray on some perfume. Siearra head towards the kitchen to butter the baked potatoes and put a little Mojo on the steaks before she replaced it back in the oven. She then got two wine glasses out and poured some light liquor inside. There's suddenly a knock on the door! Knock, knock, knock; Siearra opens the door and its Jose standing there with a card in one hand and roses in the other hand. He was wearing long blue slacks and a matching shirt and some dark blue dress shoes damn this man is fine Thought Siearra! Hello Jose, come on in; Jose steps in the door and gives Siearra a kiss on the cheek, before saying mami something smelling good; but not as good is you." When the food is finally done, they sit, eat, talk, and laugh together. Then they turn the surround sound on and make their way on to the back porch. Then Jose led Siearra out to the tropical hut where they share a few more laugh and drinks. Siearra turn towards Jose and open her robe to let him see that I had dressed for the occasion. Jose pulled her out of the chair and took the robe the rest of the way off then stepped back and licked his lips as he eyed her down. Jose sits on the floor, lay his head back on the seat of the chair and says I want you to come ride my face until your body begin to tremble and legs start shaking then cum in my mouth. Siearra does as she's instructed and place her knees in the chair and lock Jose's face in between. She's going slow at first, then as her vagina get wetter she gets more relaxed and in tune with the motion. Siearra lift her ass high to let him get some air but Jose pulls her back down quickly. She's moaning so loudly it's no wonder if the neighbors hear her hollering, her body is in an uproar of pure pleasure. She cum so quickly and he tries as a mad man to catch each and every drop. He then lay her on her stomach and spread her legs and slide his penis deeply in her vagina. Siearra slightly arch her back up and work her muscles as she's throwing her ass back. Jose pulls her up on her knees now in the doggy style position and spank her on her ass. Yes, baby she yells as he's going harder and faster within every stroke. He's squeezing her nipples and nibbling on her neck; it feels so good to her and she is loving every moment of this enjoyment. The next position was for Siearra to get on top and ride his penis. She slides down on top of his huge 9inch cock and she's going up and down while rotating her hips. He's spanking and squeezing her ass cheeks and pounding her vagina so hard it feels like its inside her stomach. Her legs are trembling, and her body is clenched into a locked riding position, she can feel all her juices flowing down. Ah baby oh baby she yells out I can't hold it no longer baby. Ah ah ah and her body tremble and her legs give out just as she cums. Jose lay her backwards and she hear him grunt just as he let out a big nut. They lay down and hold each other before making their way to the shower and making love all over the shower.

Chapter Two: Best Friend Man

He always looks at me then smile when I would walk his way. We never really said much to each other, and one night while at work he Say's I'll pay you for a dance. So, I slid between his legs and bounced my ass up and down. Now Being That I'M 5'6, 173LBS, medium breast, small waist, juicy ass, and caramel it wouldn't take much to have a man insane in seconds wanting another dance. Then I slowly drop my top and let my boobs hang out. He slightly squeezed my nipples and I turn around to face him. I realized it's my best friend boyfriend Ty. Damn I wanted to jump up and run, but something wouldn't let me. I begin to slow grind on top of Ty as his man hood began to rise I can feel it growing bigger and bigger. He's licking at my nipples and I can feel my vagina growing hot. He slides his hand across my vagina, and then Ty insert one finger, then another. Pushing deeper and deeper oh ah I moan as my juices escape my body and run down his hand. I look him in his eyes and say yes! I lift up, so he can free his rock-hard penis from his pants, so I can slide down on it. We really didn't care if anyone was watching because we were in a place of erotic ecstasy. I'm working my hips and bouncing my vagina up and down on Ty 11 ½ inch dick. He's slapping my ass cheeks with each and every thrust. Pushing his self-deeper inside my soaking wet vagina, my legs begin to grow weak as I begin to climax. Sex is so intense as a glistening rinse, our bodies intertwined in one another, then you grunt and groan as your nut shoots helplessly within me. We sit there breathless and you whisper in my ear the sex was great can we make it officially a date? I respond you are my best friend man, but yes, we definitely have to meet again at my place on Friday 8:00pm be there!

Chapter Three: Dildo Party

Susan called up some friends and said hey y'all let's have a party! Some men can come, but we don't need no men there that's going to get mad because we're using dildos. Susan friends responds on we are going to get the stuff we need for the party! Phone hangs up! Susan then sends a text to all her girlfriends about the dildo party and told them to tell a friend to tell a friend. Susan drives to the sex shop and buy different colors and sizes dildos and bullet. Along with handcuffs, sex oils, face masks, and whips to turn this party up. Susan then leaves the sex shop to go and buy drinks for the party and a vacation sweet at the holiday inn. She then set the room up with the party lights and vibrators in a basket with condoms. Then she places a bottle next to it on ice, with rose petals all over the floor. Susan then leaves to take a shower and gets dressed for the party. Susan texts her friends with the room number for the party. Susan had on a blue and pink see through long dress lingerie. Those long legs are showing due to the split in the side of the lingerie! Susan is a chocolate average size sista with thickness in all the right spots. After arriving back at the room, Susan turns the music on and makes herself a drink, when there's a knock at the door. Susan opens the door and it's about 15 people ready to party, looking all fly. After letting them in, conversations begin to roar. People start to drinking and dancing, when Susan spotted her mark. She was standing over in the corner with polo head to toe and long dreads, maybe 5'7 and 180lbs solid. Susan strolls straight towards her and introduces herself. Hello I'm Susan! What's your name, and why you standing over here all alone? I'm Sarah, but everyone calls me pop! I'm standing over here just trying to feel the vibe! That's cool replies Susan, do you want a drink and a dance? Pop replies yes! A couple drinks and dances later, Susan finds herself grinding on pop to R. Kelly song: It seems like you're ready! Pop starts slowly kissing Susan neck, and drops the top to her lingerie. Pop then begin suckling on her nipples until they're rock hard and pointed all the way out. Pop went to refill the drinks and grabbed some condoms from the table then made her way back to Susan on the bed. Susan looks around for her friends, but all she sees is ass up in the air, or legs up over shoulders. Pop laid Susan on her back and says don't worry I brought my special dildo just for you. It was pink 9inches and it was already strapped on. Pop spread Susan legs and kissed around her clit, took two fingers to spread the lips on Susan vagina open and then shoved her tongue deeply inside. Oh, how she ate the pussy so well, Susan grabbed a handful of Pop dreads! She started working her hips and arched her back in, as Pop pushes her legs up in the air and began licking on my lil man in the boat! Ah shit, oh shit, eat this pussy moans Susan! Pop then have Susan get on her knees and suck her dildo. She begins to take her fake penis slowly inside her mouth, in and out. Pop asks do you like sucking my dick don't you?! Slurp aww yes replies Susan! Pop turns Susan around and begin fucking her from the back. Susan loves to feel the thrust of Pop Strapped on dildo going in and out of her vagina. Pop's pulling Susan hair and holding her slightly up by the lower line of her stomach, as Susan body start to shake, and her juices began to escape. Susan moan out in pure pleasure as she climaxed then collapsed on the bed.

Chapter Four: Sex in the Air

I come home from a long day of work, ready to take a shower and hit the bed. I open the door to find rose petals making a path to the bedroom doorway. I followed them and find you standing there waiting for me to enter. You remove my clothes and lead me toward the bathroom, and into the shower. After I'm done showering, you then invite me into the kitchen where there are candles lit and dinner on the table. The music is playing softly as feed me and I feed you. We then move from the kitchen to the living room on the couch. You kiss me passionately that it sends chills up and down through my spine. Sex was filling up in the air, as you pull me close to you and we began to kiss more hungrily! You stick your tongue in my mouth and search lustfully until yours connect with mine. I lay on my back as you spray whipped cream on my breast, then down my stomach and all over my vagina. You grasp one breast and cup my nipple with your mouth, over and over from one to another until all the cream was gone. You then follow the trail down my belly to my spot that was oh so hot! I can feel my vagina begin to jump and grow moist as you approach with your mouth. You stop and traced my bikini line with your tongue, then slowly begin to lick the whipped cream off my vagina and with every lick I can feel your tongue getting closer and closer to my clit when suddenly you plunged your tongue into my tight vagina hole. Oh, shit baby; eat this pussy I say as I'm steadily working my hips, and then you enter two fingers inside my vagina! You're kissing and nibbling at my little man in the boat, oh yesss I repeatedly moan out. Sex in the air is all you smell a sensation of pure ecstasy. I grab your head and wrap my legs around your neck, then I arch my back a little to hold your head straight pulling your face closer and closer all while I'm working my fat juicy pussy all on your tongue. You turn me on my side, then lay on your side; next thing I feel is your tongue licking my ass hole and three fingers in my throbbing wet vagina. I jump at first then you say baby just relax, because tonight is your night. So just let me please you, okay baby! Oh, shit it feels so good, licking around then inside and out. Hell, every few minutes you stuck your finger in my ass; it felt so good while three fingers inside my vagina and fucking me in my ass with another. Just the thought of what you doing to me is making me grow week all over. You then open my pussy lips and lunged all 12inches of pure thick black dick in my pussy. Then two fingers in my ass it felt great I wanted to scream to the top of my lungs; shit, fuck yes, fuck, harder baby fuck me harder, and finger fuck me in my ass! Oh, shit yes baby damn just like that! My vagina began throbbing every time you pull it out and put it back in. You grip me tight as we both begin to climax in ecstasy; then fall fast asleep naked right there in the living room.

Chapter Five: Sleeping with the Judge!

Tami was always the type of girl who stayed in and out of jail, every time you turned around it was always something she did to always have her in court. Then one day all that just seemed to change;

Here's Her Story:

Girl I'm so tired of having to bring you back and forth to court, is this every going to stop?! Asks Toni"

Tami replies girl I try to stay out of trouble but for some reason it always seems to find me, and this time I got three more court dates after this one, but I promise you Toni I'll try my hardest to stay out of trouble. Now are you going to listen to what happened or not Toni?

Toni replies yes go head

Tami: I walked into the court room and soon as the judge walked in everyone stood up and he motioned for us to take our seats. I noticed that he was kind of handsome sitting up there behind the bench, occasionally, ill glance up there to see him looking at me through his eye glasses. Damn I began to get moist between the legs every time I looked up to see his juicy dark pink lips. Then I heard my name being called, so I get up and I dressed in long black silk like material pants with red and white stripes going down them and a red long-sleeved shirt with matching shoes. Girl my hair was black and red with deep curls in it. So, I start approaching the podium, but I could feel the judge deep stare on me and my nipples stuck straight forward. I ended up having to stay after court, that's when I had told you to leave because I was going to catch a ride or call you back to get me if I couldn't get one. So anyway, girl once court was over the judge asked to see me in his chambers. When I entered his chambers, he takes his robe and I almost fainted, damn he was no more than 5'6 and weighed a 200 solid. He had really nice curly hair and his skin color looked as if it was just tanned. The judge closed chamber doors and locked it and then says you're one beautiful young lady. I noticed that you have three more court dates and I'll be the judge! I was a bit confused until the judge said well if you agree to sleep with me whenever I want it I'll make all these problems go away. I could dismiss the charges, but before you jump off the handle I'll give you an allowance or help pay a bill if you need it, but I must warn you sometimes I may get lonely and want you to spend the night with me, go to the movies, take trips, go out to eat but if any of my colleagues bump into us, we will just try to play it off or say we are on a business meeting for an interview. The judge then walks up close to me and kiss me on my forehead, then ask so do we have a deal. Bad as I wanted to say no for some reason I couldn't because I wanted to see the dick he had between his legs and wondered if it was good or not. Yes, your honor I agree! So, the judge says well here's your first assignment, come over here and get on your knees then suck my dick! So, I walk around his desk and unbuckled his belt and then waits for my prize, when he pulled out his 10inch super fat penis my eyes almost popped out my head. I grasped his nut sack with one hand and slowly started stroking his penis with the other hand. I feel it began to grow hard, so I slid it in my mouth and released my hand from around it. I began sucking the judge penis slightly hard and fast, he then placed his hand around my head and started guiding me up and down on it. It was so huge I could feel myself beginning to choke that's when the judge says don't stop keep sucking my dick. He then starts to fuck my mouth while tightly pulling my hair as he's moving my head back and forth while grunting oh shit suck this dick. I thought he was trying to put it down my throat, but I kept right on sucking it. I heard him say damn I'm about to nut, swallow my cum and I mean every bit of it. So about three pumps later Toni girl he held my head steady and then came in my mouth, and I swallowed it. After we were done I left out and started walking because he was going to pick me up from down the road. The next time we hooked up was like four days before my next court date, girl it was a Saturday night when the judge picked me up and took me back to the courthouse. Now I like hell no I'm not supposed to be here on a Saturday night! We go up to the second floor and he goes to enter the courtroom. Once we get inside I immediately grow nervous, because I'm like what if any one come and catch us here. He said baby relax I'm going to take care of you! I'm dressed in this black and gold dress with my breast area open and my see through black laced bra showing. I have on a black laced thong with gold around the rim (also see through black and gold stocking and black high heels) my hair was straight sowed in also black and gold with gold accessories to match the outfit. The judge is dressed in a blue and black expensive suit and it looks like he's been trimmed up. His polo cologne is lingering in the air, mixing into my Victoria's secret love spell perfume. I say you honor! If you don't mind me asking what is your nationality? He smiles and replies I'm black and Indian. Well how old are you I then asked? He says baby I'm forty-three, is that a problem?! Don't forget about our deal because you still have to come see me in court, I haven't thrown the case out yet and if you think you're going to try and bail out after I drop one you have another thing coming. I have been recording the whole conversation just to have a little insurance he says as he picks up the picnic basket and pulled out a bottle of wine and poured us some as he fed me fruits. Then the judge started kissing on my neck and it was beginning to get me hot. He freed my nipples from my bra and dropped my dress on the floor. We then walked over to the jury stand and took a seat as he starts to get on his knees. He kissed my nipples and slid his penis inside my tight vagina I gasp and whisper ooo shit your dick is so big as begin to stroke my vagina. He stops and pulls me to the edge and lay me back till I can feel my back slightly touching the seat. He pushed his penis back inside my throbbing wet vagina and started stroking me over and over I softly begin to moan yes yes shit yes fuck me your honor harder and harder. He grabs a handful of my hair and snatches my head backwards and then start kissing up my stomach. I can feel his juicy penis deep inside my vagina till it almost seemed to be in the bottom of my stomach. I'm throwing my pussy back its feeling so good he's whispering in my ear you like that don't you, I yell out yes, I like it. He grabs me and take me out to the bench where we sit if were waiting on our name to be called, the judge then takes me down to the edge and tell me to get on my knees and lay the top of my body on the bench then spread my legs apart. I do as I'm instructed, and he plunged his fat cock inside of me and squeezed my hips then asked me if this how I want it. I said yes baby and I want it rough, so the judge is fucking me from the back as rough as he possibly could. Spanking my ass cheeks, I can feel myself about to masturbate. I'm throwing my pussy back and were both moaning and groaning. My legs begin to tremble, so I grab a tight hold of the bench; I'm shaking and moaning so loudly as I begin to catch my organism. He cuffs his hands around my waist and pounds and pound until he unloads his cum deeply inside of me. That's when we hear the door click as if someone was watching. A week later the judge started receiving black mail calls because they had found out I was sleeping with the judge.

Chapter Six: The Hospital Room

I rush home from work; grab a couple things from the house before I head to the hospital to see my friend John because I received a phone call saying he's been admitted in the hospital. So, I rush over to the bed and say john I came as soon as I heard you was here. He turns over and say now you know you did not have to do that, I just had a bad headache and felt a little dizzy. I respond you know I always had a little crush on you, but anyway while I'm here do you need me to help you with anything. John 6'1 220lbs chocolate long hair and a mouth full of gold. He says yes, I need you to come help me with this, I then respond help you with what!? John says this, as he pulls the covers back I see nothing but a 12inch fat, thick penis hanging out. I hurry to close the hospital room door and slide the curtains closed so no one could see inside. Then I tell him john lay back as I slowly begin to unbutton my shirt and let it drop to the floor. John says damn girl you got my dick standing tall, come on over here and let me kiss on them sexy nipples. I walk over to the side of the bed and say are you sure about this because I don't want the machines to start going off. John laughs and say come on up here! I get on top lift my skirt and pull my panties over to the side. He grabs my both hands slightly pinching at y nipples. So, I lean forward until his lips meet up with my breast and he began to suckle on them as if he was waiting on some milk to squirt out. I grab his penis and easily start to slide down on it. Shit baby this pussy tight and wet, I'm going to take it slow okay don't worry. I then respond ok as I continue to try and get all his cock in my vagina. He gently began to easily push back oh yes, I moan out damn john you dick is so big. Finally, it's all the way inside my vagina I scream out shit yes fuck me john. He grabs me under my ass cheeks and holds them apart while he's pounding my insides with all his might. I lean backward and lock my hands on his thighs while riding his penis up and down real fast. John grabs my waist and pulls me forward then began kissing on my neck, I feel my vagina tightening then losing up as he's at a steady slow-paced thrust. I can feel john at my spot and I'm about to cum. I kiss him on the neck over and over as I'm riding up and down, he says baby hold on you're going to make me cum! No, I whisper in his ear"! I'm about to cum as I squeeze the bed with both hands, I moan oh john damn this dick so good, I'm coming, and he then spanks me on my ass cheeks, my legs are shaking, and my vagina is soaking wet the covers are getting wet from my juices flowing down. John then grunts and groan damn breathing husky damn and he pull me up and open my ass cheeks and nut right in between them. Damn girl you got some good pussy hell I think you just cured me. We both laugh I kissed him on the lips then says well I'm going to get dressed to go, call me if you need anything. I'll come back and check on you later about 9:00 and hopefully you be in a room already. Ok says john and I got dressed and left.

Chapter Seven: Three Way Sex

Hey bae I yell! I'm in the back-room bae, he yells back. I walk in the room and say Brian I was wondering how would you feel about me and another woman? Niecy stop playing with me girl I know you not serious! Niecy was 5'4 bowlegged average size sexy chick! I respond Brian I'm not playing hell I see the way these chicks look at you who wouldn't? shit you're 6'0 tall about 210lbs with dreds gold and he's dark skinned; muscular and always stay swagged out. He just laughs you tripping girl, but I'll be back later I got to make a run across town with my boys. Ok bae I respond as he kisses me on the cheek and head out the door. I pick my phone up and dial up Lola who I met about a month ago at a party I hosted, and she was one of the dancers. Shawty was stacking hell she was Dominican 5'5 185lbs 36b small waist long hair and an ass like Jackie-o! damn lil babie was fine. I get her to slide through and kick it with me for a while.

An hour later after chatting and catching up on the gossip, I say Lola how about us going to get in the Jacuzzi? Sure, replies Lola and play some music while you're at it. So, I turn on some music first song to come on was beat it up by 50 cent and Lola was already undressed getting into the hot tub. Damn that ass was fat, I couldn't help but think how pretty this girl was, and it just had me in a gaze. Um hello, Lola voice interrupted my thoughts, are you getting in today? I drop my clothes to the floor and get in with her and now she's bouncing her ass up and down. I say damn Lola that ass fat you don't mind me touching it do you? I thought you'd never ask Niecy you can touch whatever you like she say as she make her way over to me and sit on my lap. I'm nervous as I squeeze one cheek then the other I take a long sip of my Alize and light up my blunt I had rolled up. We finished smoking when sex is on my mind started playing on the radio, then Lola leaned and over and kissed me. I must have gotten really hot because next thing you know we are kissing and sucking on each other neck, licking on each other breast, so I say let's go to the kitchen counter. After entering the kitchen, I grab the phone and calls Brian. Hello, he answers, I then say bae I need you to the house right now it's an emergency. Brian replies alright I'll be there in 20minutes okay! Okay bae hurry I yell! Lola smiles then she drops to her knees and spread my legs then proceeds to sticking her tongue in my growing wet vagina. Um yes, I moan out softly stop let's go to the bed. Now once in the bed Lola says you just spread my vagina lips and lick with your tongue but not too hard and not too soft. Ok I say as we lay down. She then gets on top of me and open her legs I then take my fingers and part her lips and begin to kiss then lick her vagina as she moans yes baby you got it. Now Lola is sliding her fingers inside my vagina that's burning with sensation while licking my little man in the boat. I moan louder ahh yes oh ahh yes, that's when the room door swings open and Brian yells damn what the fuck is going on in here?! Let me sit down and watch y'all says Brian as he starts getting undressed. Bae who is this? Well her name is oh wait oh um shit ah…. Lola that's her name! Brian is now standing naked at the end of the bed stroking his 9 1/2-inch dick. Can I join shit y'all making my dick harder than a bitch?! Yes, we both yelled out and he starts to eat my pussy with Lola, then he lays Lola down beside me and begins to kiss her pussy lips. He lays us with our legs crossed over one another and start to go from her pussy to mine licking and suckling. Lola and I are kissing each other while Brian has two fingers in both our vaginas licking us up and down all over our bodies. He lay in the bed and we both kiss his dick as he makes it jump. We then lick up both sides of his cock, I then start to work my way down and capture his nut sack inside my mouth. Lola is sucking Brian dick while he is eating her pussy. Then Lola lies down, and I began to eat her rose smelling pussy and Brian fucks me doggy style. There's moaning, groaning, ass smacking and pleasure cries in the air. Once again, we switch positions and now I'm lying down, and Lola is giving me head and Brian is now fucking her doggy style. I grab the back of Lola head and push her face closer as I feel myself begin to climax. I look up at Brian to find him in a deep stare at me; we lock eyes and next thing you know I'm working my pussy holding her head just fucking her face while my man is fucking the shit out of her. I begin to moan still staring at him, oooohhh shit fuccck yes aahh shit I moaned with a trimly voice. Brian still staring at me stroking Lola from behind, Lola says papi, yes papi you make me cum papi she screams as she buries her head in the pillow body trembling then G say both y'all come over here and open your mouth. Brian began to jack off and about two minutes later he shoots his nutt in the both of our mouths.

Chapter Eight: Licking His Ass

Most men say they will never let a woman lick his ass and most women says hell no they wouldn't even attempt to do nothing like that, that's disgusting to even think about. Well I say never say never; here's the story...

Jacob was 5'9 190lbs light skinned honey brown eyes very athletic sexy lips and a nice clean cut. We would always go to the club to dance drink and just chill out. Then one night while we were out partying Jacob says Mariah you're so fine 5'4 dark skinned fat ass parrot toed pretty brown eyes damn you sexy. You keep backing that ass up on me and you're going to get in trouble. I smile and keep dancing, Jacob begin to kiss my neck then lick around my ear, I could feel his nature getting big in his pants, so I start popping and grinding my ass all over him. We drink some more, then we leave for my house to see how the rest of the night will turn out. Now back at my two-bedroom apartment Jacob and I takes a shower and wash each other body. We make our way to the bedroom and I lay him face down on the bed ad start massaging him. I then spread his ass cheeks apart then take my finger and rub it up the crack of his ass. Jacob fidgets a little, so I stop and say are you ok? I don't want you to feel like I'm violating you because this is something for pleasure and you got to be relaxed. Jacob replies ok baby I'm cool! I begin licking down his back and when I got to his buttocks I blew. I then trace circles around his asshole; he then tightened up again but soon relaxed quickly. I then took my finger and slightly begin to play with his ass while still licking between his cheeks. I grasp his nut sack with my other free hand, and Jacob moans slightly but firmly so I begin to slide my finger little by little in his ass and then swirl it a little. I'm sucking one nut then the other before licking up the base of his penis, Jacob begin to grunt out loud damn girl as I'm sucking his cock swallowing it deep in and out of my throat. He grabs my head and pushes his penis as deep in mouth as he could before unloading his cum in my mouth for me to swallow. Jacob and I then lay there cuddling until we fell asleep.

Chapter Nine: Icee Pleasure

Megan loved to party and always was wild. She loved to show her sexy bowlegs and loved miniskirts. Megan was 5'3 145lbs apple sized breast with a Nia Long ass and full-blooded Haitian. One day her friends were asking her would she go to this lingerie hotel pool party, which was about 5days away from Sunday. Megan replies hell yea I'm going, I wonder who all will be there. Now the day of the party has arrived and Megan dresses in this netted tiger lingerie suit where the pussy area was free, and she had on black thongs, a mask, hooker heels and her whip. When she arrived at the party things were just heating up, and Megan walks inside where she finds her girlfriends taking shots. Megan joined the party, and it doesn't take long for her to notice this Dominican papi across the room. Damn he got swag racking some pants, and a red and black matching shit, to top it all off, He had a red hat with black writing that said (I'm A Freak). Megan could see him staring her down and licking his juicy lips! He walks over and says hello I'm Hector lets step into the dining room with me, so we can talk in private. Then she replied Hector my name is Megan and sure we can talk. We then enter the dining room, where we take a seat on a futon and have some more drinks. Suddenly Hector says let me rub on your sexy body. Megan allow Hector to slide her clothes off, and he lays her down on her back, then he takes an ice cube, and sit it in her belly button as the ice cube slowly began to melt, Hector would kiss and lick up the water, as it slowly rolls down Megan's body. She shivers a little bit, then Hector places an ice cube in his mouth and slowly began to caress Megan's vagina! Hector is now massaging Megan vagina with his mouth. (oooh shit papi yes, I like it) moaned Megan, Hector then grabs Megan pulls her onto his lap where he easily slides his huge cock into Megan's already soaked vagina. Slowly he began to push deep into Megan's vagina while she's on top. Hector spanks Megan ass, o yes papi she softly moans out! Megan feel her organism about to come, so she wraps her arms around hector neck and curved her back straddling him down while popping her vagina until she climaxed!

Chapter Ten: Getting Buck Wild

Tiffany jumps out the shower and run to the phone! Hello yes, I'm cuming I'm trying to get dressed, a short while later tiffany jumps in the car with her friends and pull off. They pull up to the house get out and go to the door, once inside things start to turn up! Everyone is everywhere drinking, smoking, popping molly, etc. Tiffany grabs a glass of gin and pineapple juice then go off to find something to get into, but not before popping a molly. Tiffany finds herself out by the pool with a girl kissing and making out. The girl began sucking on tiffany breast, caressing each with her mouth. She pulls off tiffany underwear while wasting no time pushing her tongue inside tiffany vagina! So passionately with each lick she gives as she is tasting my sweet juices. Then she turns and puts her vagina on tiffany lips and say suck this pussy. Now they're doing the 69ner; sliding their fingers in and out of each other's vagina. The pleasure escaping into the air, tiffany began to pull the pussy back to where she's fucking with her tongue and next thing she came!

Chapter eleven: On your head upside down!

Slim always seem to catch slick on the same corner, every day she walked by. Now there's nothing wrong with slim accept slick assumed that he was a dope boy because he had on some fresh Jordan shoes, black Levi (pants with the crease) and one of those shirts with the quotes on the front, but the whole outfit matched the shoes. Slim was 5'9 and weighed about 150lbs with gold teeth, he was cleaned cut with dark honey brown eyes, black & Jamaican. Slick didn't care that he was fine with money; she just didn't want a dope boy. Slick was 5'6, 175lbs, hazel eyes caramel with a Haitian accent. Slim grabbed slick hand and said damn baby girl every day you walk past here, and I ask you to let me take you to dinner! Slick responds look man I keep telling you I don't want to be involved with a drug dealer. Slim laughs and say baby I work and the only reason I be out here is because I be waiting on you to walk by! Why don't you just let me take you to dinner and we could get to know each other better, Slick says okay pick me up at 8:00pm! Later that night Slick steps out the door to find Slim standing next to a 2012 Mercedes Benz with a dozen of roses. Slick says thank you as Slim hands her the flowers and closes the car door for her. He then jumps into the car and says I'm taking you to this jazz club and the food is great you will love it! After leaving the club and returning home, Slick invites Slim inside for a drink, that's when he grabs her and say I don't mean to be rude but it something I really want to do to your body. They start to kiss slowly as Slim rubs his hands down her body. He then lays Slick gently on the bed and slowly removes her clothes. Slick shivers at the touch of Slim lips kissing from her neck all the way down to her navel and then to her panty line. Slim slowly traces Slick pussy with his tongue and then without warning he begins to fuck her with his tongue. Slick moans loudly as Slim makes his way slowly kissing and licking her ass. Slim steadily Caressed Slick from the front to the back; Slim then lay Slick on her stomach where her head is hanging towards the edge of the bed and begin to gently inch his huge fat 10 ½ inch penis inside her tight wet and throbbing vagina. The doggy style position was Slick's favorite position but just as they were getting into the motion and grove; Slick decides to throw Slim a curve ball to see just how far he would go. She slid off the edge of the bed, put her arms and head on the floor propped herself up with her legs straight up in the air. Slim said so you freaky huh? So, this is what you really want to do, we going to do it say Slim as he stands over Slick and wraps his arms around her waist and spreads her legs into a v! He slides his erect love muscle inside Slick's soak and wet tunnel of love, then he slowly pounds her tunnel of love; slick says harder baby I like it rough! Slim pounds deeply and with every hard thrust, slick lets out a loud moan. Slick legs begin buckle as she cries out in pleasure just as she reaches her climax and Slim grunts as he reaches his peak. Then they shower and fall fast asleep!

Conclusion: Dripping Wet

Carla sits around and fantasizes about what sex would be like if Nate the stud gave her the chance! Many times, Carla find herself stuck in a daydream about coming out the shower in only a towel and walking into the bedroom where Nate was waiting with the lights dimmed low. Carla slowly makes her way over to the bed where Nate then laid her down and lotion her body. The sensation of each touch made Carla tunnel of love throb and grow moist. They begin to passionately kissing and then Nate pulls out her 12inch strap and says can you handle it? Carla replies don't ask just come put it on me and find out. Nate slowly slides her strapped fake dick inside Carla now soaked vagina. That's when a screen door slammed, and Carla stopped daydreaming as she realized her pussy was dripping wet.

Thank you for taking the time out to read my book; I really hope you enjoyed it as much as I enjoyed writing it.

To my fans: I appreciate your love and support

Find me: Www.Facebook.com/AuthorHubert

Email: L.Shelton212@gmail.Com

Author Lakyshia

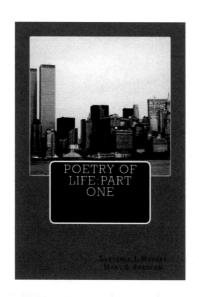

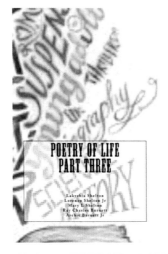

POETRY OF LIFE
PART THREE

Lakyshia Shelton
Lorenzo Shelton Jr
Mary L Shelton
Ray Charles Burnett
Archie Burnett Jr

Let's Help Each Other
*Can You Relate To
These Stories*

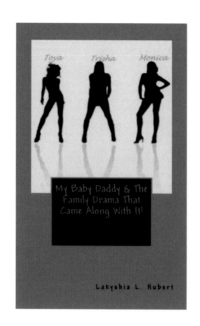

More coming soon!

Made in the USA
Columbia, SC
01 March 2021